U0065150

To my niece and nephew,

Maya and Milan

Paulo Joins the Fleet

第一次捕魚

Christian Beamish 著

吳泳霈 譯

朱正明 繪

Stars were still glimmering over the palm trees on the island of Santiago in Cape Verde when Paulo walked down the path to the beach with his father and older brother, Enrique. Paulo hardly slept the night before because today was the first day that the boy would go to sea. He was nervous and excited. The other fishermen were already on the beach and they sat cross-legged on the sand next to their boats, baiting hooks and coiling lines by the light of their small glass lanterns.

Paulo's brother Enrique thought that Paulo was still too young to accompany them to go fishing. "Paulo can't work; he'll get cold and cry," he said the previous evening.

"All the other boats have only two fishermen," Paulo's father said. He smiled and lifted Paulo into his arms, "But with Paulo, we'll have two and a half!"

Paulo smiled and said, "You'll see, Enrique, I'll be able to fish."

Enrique shook his head, stood up and walked away.

Paulo was determined to learn and to be helpful. He heaved the lines into the boat and waded into the cold water to launch the skiff, and climbed up over the side like all the other fishermen.

Still, Enrique criticized him. “You’re rocking the boat!” he yelled when Paulo climbed in. “Don’t knock over that line!” he said angrily when Paulo stepped over the coils to sit.

Paulo’s father arranged gear in the bow area and didn’t say anything about Enrique’s behavior toward his little brother.

The sun was rising now and the sky looked pink in the first light of day.

There were three other boats in the water and the fishermen shouted to be heard over the growling of outboard motors.

“Hey Enrique!” one of the fishermen called out. “Is that little Paulo going fishing with you?”

“That’s right,” Enrique shouted back.

“But the fish weigh more than he does!” the fisherman replied and the other men laughed.

“I’m big enough,” Paulo said, but no one seemed to hear him.

“You’ll make me the laughing stock of the fleet!” Enrique snarled as he yanked the pull-cord to the motor.

The outboard motor growled to life and a bluish puff of smoke rose behind the skiff and Paulo, his father and his brother Enrique followed the other boats. The fishing boats stayed close together until they reached the south tip of the island where the lighthouse stood. The fishing boats then separated when they went out to the open ocean.

Paulo turned to look for his friend Joaquim the lighthouse keeper, but they were already too far out for the boy to see anything other than the shape of the lighthouse tower. The other boats were far away now and they looked like toys on the vast face of the sea. Paulo pulled his cap down tighter and wrapped his arms around himself against the chill morning air.

They motored on and on, further and further out to sea. The skiff raced over the water and Paulo felt the wind on his face and the sun beginning to warm his shoulders. In the distance, Paulo, his father and Enrique saw hundreds of birds flying and diving into the sea.

"Go there!" Paulo's father told Enrique.

Enrique made the skiff go fast over the water to where the birds were feeding. The birds were flying overhead now and the sea looked like it was boiling with the slashing and cutting of the fish on the surface.

"Out of the way, Paulo!" Enrique yelled as he scrambled to get his line in the water.

Paulo's father also rushed to his line, feeding it out hand over hand, the baited hooks flipping over the rail one after the next.

Paulo grabbed a line and threw it into the water like his father and brother had done.

Enrique told Paulo, "You don't know how to fish!" as he brought in the first sleek, blue tuna.

Then Paulo felt a tug on his line and the boy pulled back sharply and pulled in his own sleek tuna, silvery underneath with its big eye staring skyward.

"That's the way, Paulo!" his father shouted, smiling broadly. "His fish was as big as yours, Enrique!" Paulo's father said, laughing.

They fished all afternoon. The cool air of morning gave way to hot sunshine burning down on Paulo, his father and his brother. The fishing line cut Paulo's hands and the saltwater stung in his wounds every time Paulo brought a fish in. But Paulo would not complain. He did not want Enrique to think that he was weak, so Paulo kept fishing throughout the day, baiting hooks and pulling in tuna just like his father and his older brother. Paulo's shoulders ached and the cuts on his hands stung, but still the boy continued to fish.

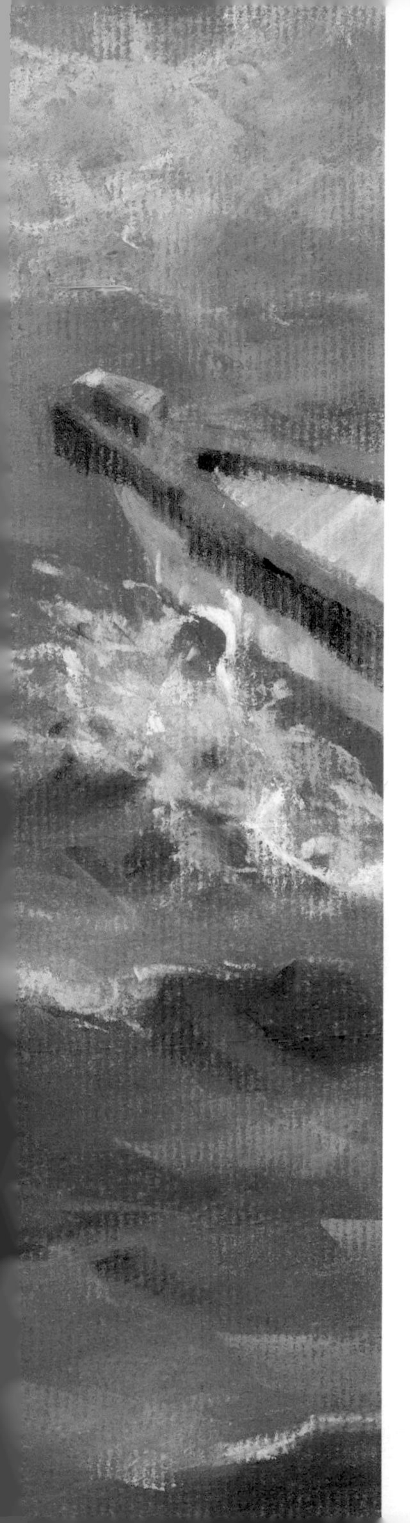

Finally, the time came to go in. The fish they had caught lay in the bottom of the skiff like chopped firewood and as the skiff motored to shore, Paulo watched the island and looked for the lighthouse tower. When Enrique landed the skiff on the beach, the other fishermen came down to help them. Small waves crashed on the shore, the sunlight sparkled on the water. They unloaded and weighed their catch.

"How did little Paulo do out there today?" one of the fishermen asked the boy's father.

"He did very well," Paulo's father said smiling, putting his hand on Paulo's shoulder.

The only thing that Paulo wanted to do was sleep.

The man at the scale announced that Paulo, his father and Enrique had caught more fish than any other boat that day.

The fishermen cheered. One of them slapped Paulo on the back. “Good job, Paulo!” he said.

Someone else said, “Congratulations.”

“But the fish weigh more than he does!” another gravelly voice said in admiration and the fishermen all laughed.

As Paulo, his father and Enrique walked home up the path from the beach, Enrique said, “Good job today, Paulo, I’m proud of you. Welcome to the fleet.”

Paulo shook hands with his brother and smiled.

Vocabulary

fleet [flit] n. 船隊

P.3

glimmer [`glɪmɚ] v. 閃爍不定

coil [kɔɪl] v. 把……捲成圈狀

P.6

heave [hiv] v. 將（重物）舉起、提起

wade [wed] v. 涉水而行

skiff [skɪf] n. 小艇

coil [kɔɪl] n. 一捲（線等）

P.9

growl [graʊl] n. 轟隆聲

outboard motor　船尾馬達

P.11

laughing stock 笑柄

snarl [snɑrl] v. 咆哮著說

yank [jæŋk] v. 猛拉，拉扯

P.13

bluish [`bluɪʃ] adj. 帶藍色的

puff [pʌf] n. 一股，一陣

P.18

slash [slæʃ] v. 砍

scramble [`skræmbḷ] v. 倉促行動

flip [flɪp] v. 翻轉

rail [rel] n. 橫桿

P.20

grab [græb] v. 抓起

sleek [slik] adj. 有光澤的

tuna [`tunə] n. 鮪魚

underneath [ˌʌndɚ`niθ] adv. 在下面

P.25

unload [ʌn`lod] v. 從（車、船等）卸下貨物

P.26

scale [skel] n. 磅秤

P.29

slap [slæp] v. 拍打

gravelly [`grævəlɪ] adj. 聲音粗啞的

故事中譯

P.3

當星星仍然在維德角聖地牙哥島的棕櫚樹上方閃爍時，保羅已和爸爸還有哥哥安立奎走在通往海灘的小路上。今天是保羅第一次出海捕魚的日子，緊張和興奮的心情，讓他前一天晚上幾乎無法入睡。其他漁夫們早已到了海邊，他們盤著腿坐在船邊的沙灘上，在一盞盞小型玻璃提燈的微光下，將魚餌裝上釣勾，把漁線捲繞成圈。

P.4

保羅的哥哥安立奎認為保羅還太小，根本不適合和他們一起出海捕魚。前一天晚上他還說:「保羅做不了這份工作的啦!他一定會冷得受不了,然後哭出來的。」

保羅的父親說：「其他漁船都只有兩個漁夫。但是有了保羅，我們就有兩個半了！」他微笑著將保羅舉起抱進懷裡。

保羅笑著說：「等著瞧吧，安立奎，我一定能捕到魚的。」

安立奎搖搖頭，起身走開。

P.6

保羅下定決心要好好學習，成為有用的一員。他把漁線提起來放進船裡，然後在冰冷的水裡涉水前進，好將船推下水，再像其他的漁夫們一樣，從船的一邊爬上來。

但是安立奎還是不斷的批評他。在保羅爬進船內時，他吼著：「你讓船搖個不停！」而保羅跨過綑好的漁線要坐下時，他又生氣的說：「不要撞倒那綑漁線！」

保羅的父親在船頭整理工具，對於安立奎對弟弟的態度，他一句話也沒說。

P.8

太陽漸漸升起來了，天空在第一道曙光的照射下，暈染成一片粉紅。

P.9

水面上另外三艘漁船的漁夫，在船尾馬達隆隆作響的聲音中，大聲的喊著說話。

P.11

其中一個漁夫大叫：「嘿！安立奎！小保羅也要跟你們一起出海捕魚嗎？」

安立奎喊回去說：「是啊！」

那位漁夫回答：「可是魚都比他重了！」其他人都笑了。

保羅說：「我已經夠大了！」但似乎沒人聽見他說的話。

安立奎一邊用力拉馬達的拉繩，一邊咆哮著說：「你會害我變成船隊裡的笑柄！」

P.13

船尾馬達像又活起來似的隆隆作響，然後一陣藍煙就從小艇的後方冒出；保羅、爸爸和哥哥安立奎跟在其他漁船後方。所有的漁船緊緊靠在一起航行，直到抵達小島的南端，也就是燈塔座落的地方為止。來到外海後，漁船便分散開來。

P.14

保羅轉身尋找他的朋友——燈塔看守人喬昆，但他們已經離燈塔很遠了，除了燈塔的輪廓外，保羅什麼也看不到。其他的漁船現在也都開得很遠，它們在廣闊的海面上看起來就像玩具一樣。保羅將他的帽子往下拉緊，並用雙臂裹住身子，以阻擋清晨的寒風。

P.16

他們繼續開著船駛向更遠的海域。小艇在水上全速航行，保羅感覺到海風拂過他的臉頰，而陽光正開始溫暖他的肩膀。保羅、爸爸跟安立奎看見遠方有上百隻鳥飛著，正往海裡俯衝。

保羅的父親告訴安立奎：「到那裡去！」

P.18

安立奎加快小艇的速度，往鳥群覓食的地點前進。現在，鳥兒在他們的頭頂上飛著；由於魚群在海面不停的穿梭，大海看起來就像沸騰的開水一樣。

安立奎急急忙忙將漁線放入水中，並大叫：「保羅，讓開！」

保羅的父親也衝去拿他的漁線，一手接著一手將漁線放到海裡，掛著餌的魚鉤就一個接一個翻過船圍。

P.20

保羅模仿爸爸和哥哥，也抓起一條漁線拋進水中。

當安立奎拉起第一條富有光澤的藍色鮪魚時，他告訴保羅：「你根本不懂怎麼捕魚！」

接著，保羅感覺到他的漁線被扯了一下，於是他迅速的往後一拉，拉起了他自己捕到的鮪魚：牠有著銀色的肚皮，大大的眼睛直瞪著天空。

爸爸露出了大大的笑容，喊著：「保羅，就是這樣！」然後他笑著對安立奎說：「安立奎，他的魚和你的一樣大呢！」

P.23

他們整個下午都在捕魚。早晨的涼意早已散去，而炙熱的陽光像火焰般燃燒著保羅、爸爸以及哥哥。漁線割傷了保羅的雙手，每當他拉起一條魚，傷口就因接觸到海水而刺痛不已。但保羅並沒有抱怨。他不想讓安立奎認為他軟弱，所以整天持續不斷的捕魚、像父親和哥哥那樣在魚鉤上掛餌、拉起捕到的鮪魚。保羅覺得肩膀酸疼、手上的傷口也刺痛著，但他仍然繼續捕魚。

P.25

終於，回航的時間到了。他們捕獲的魚全部放置在小船的底部，看起來像極了劈好的薪柴。當小艇漸漸往岸邊開近的時候，保羅往島上望去，找尋燈塔的位置。安立奎將小艇停上沙灘後，其他的漁夫都過來幫忙。小浪拍打著岸邊，陽光照得水面閃閃發光。他們卸下漁獲並秤重量。

P.26

其中一位漁夫問男孩的父親：「小保羅今天在海上的表現如何啊？」

保羅的父親將手放到保羅的肩膀上，微笑著說：「他表現得非常好！」

而保羅心裡唯一想的，就是大睡一覺。

秤重的男人宣布保羅他們當天捕到的魚，比其他的漁船都還要多。

P.29

漁夫們歡呼著。其中一位拍拍保羅的背，說：「保羅，做得好！」

另一個人則說：「恭喜啊！」

此時有個沙啞的聲音用讚賞的語氣說：「魚可是都比他重喔！」所有的漁夫都笑了。

P.30

在保羅、父親及安立奎從海邊走回家的路上，安立奎說：「保羅，你今天表現得很棒！我真以你為榮。歡迎加入船隊！」

保羅和他的哥哥握了握手，臉上洋溢著微笑。

Exercises

Part One. Reading Comprehension

_____ 1. Paulo hardly slept the night before because _____.

(A) he was having a headache

(B) he was nervous and excited about going to the sea

(C) today was the first day of school for him

(D) today was the first day he went to the beach

_____ 2. Why didn't Enrique like Paulo to go fishing with them?

(A) Because he was worried about Paulo's safety.

(B) Because he was afraid Paulo would catch more fish than he did.

(C) Because he thought Paulo was too young to be helpful.

(D) Because the boat would be too small for three people.

_____ 3. What did Paulo's father mean when he said that the other boats had only two fishermen, but with Paulo, they would have two and a half?

(A) He meant Paulo was a help for fishing.

(B) He meant Paulo was not yet a fisherman.

(C) He meant their boat would be more crowded than the other boats.

(D) He meant their boat was better than the other boats.

Part Two. Topics for Discussion

Answer the following questions in your own words and try to support your answers with details in the story. There are no correct answers to the questions in this section.

1. "*But the fish weigh more than he does!*" Paulo first heard it from one fisherman before they went out for fishing, and then heard it again from another one after they came back with their catch. The two fishermen didn't seem to mean the same thing. Explain what they each meant and why they said that.
2. At the beginning, Enrique didn't want Paulo to go fishing with them, but at the end of the day, he recognized Paulo as one of their team. What made Enrique change his attitude?

Answers

Part One. Reading Comprehension

1.(B) 2.(C) 3.(A)

維德角的漁民生活

「我無法對海洋有任何怨懟，因為我所擁有的全來自海洋。」
(“I cannot hold a grudge against the sea,
because all that I have the sea has given me.”)

——維德角諺語

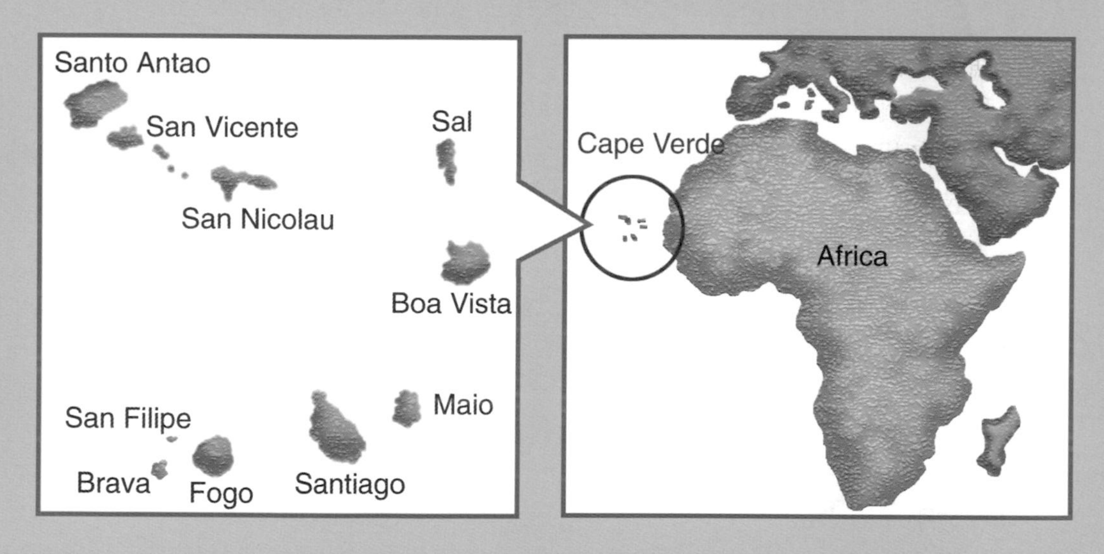

維德角共和國 (Republic of Cape Verde)，一個位處北大西洋西非洲突出部分之外海的島國，主要由十個大小島嶼組成，首都為聖地牙哥島 (Santiago) 上的培亞 (Praia)。該國原為葡萄牙殖民地，於 1975 年才獲獨立，國名即源自葡萄牙語 “Cabo Verde”，意指「綠色角落」。人口約有四十七萬兩千人，多為黑白混血。

被海洋圍繞的維德角，雖然人民多半從事農業 (佔 80%)，但是它的文化、歷史、音樂、詩歌，無一不受海洋影響。而維德角的漁民對海洋更是有一份特殊的情感，他們毫不畏懼它的變化無常，而是樂天知命的過著討海的生活。儘管海面的能見度只有幾公尺，只要沒有下雨，他們也會往海裡去──如果他們沒有喝酒醉倒的話。酒與刺青是漁民們生活最大的樂趣，維德角的漁民，很少不喝酒或沒有刺青的，這也多少反應他們隨意的生活態度。漁村裡的男孩，多半跟著爸爸學習捕魚的技巧，或是給村裡捕魚技術一流的師傅當學徒。對漁村裡的每個家庭來說，學會靠海維生算是男孩變成男人的成年禮，象徵了獨立、自尊與優秀。

維德角漁民所擁有的船隻，多為長 4-8 公尺，寬 1.6 公尺的簡陋木船，漁民多半能熟練的利用海風和三角帆 (lanteen sail) 來控制船行方向。然而，現今的船隻已有一半改為馬達發動，這種操縱三角帆的技術就逐漸在新世代裡失傳。儘管如此，要成為一個優秀的漁夫，仍要具備許多技巧。維德角漁民的一天，多半以觀察大自然為開始，一個有經驗的漁夫，會根據觀察到的大自然現象，來判斷當天的天候狀況或是漁獲量。當天若是吹東北風，空氣將會比較乾燥；若是吹南風，就很可能會遇上暴風雨；若要捕獲淺水魚，早晨與黃昏是最好的時機；若要獵捕深水魚，時間反而不重要，而是要注意潮汐與洋流……。這一切捕魚的常識，都得靠長年累月不斷在海裡征討才能習得。

時至今日，國際觀光產業逐漸在維德角扎根，這些漁民樂天的臉孔，也一一出現在飯店的旅遊手冊或明信片上，吸引來自英國、德國、或歐洲其他各地的觀光客前往。但是，在國際大型船隊的強勢入侵下，許多人開始擔心維德角的漁民將會遭受影響，他們呼籲當地政府能正視漁民的困境，改善漁民生活，否則，也許在不久的將來，我們就只能在旅遊手冊或明信片上，追憶維德角這種特殊的漁村風情了。

About the Author

Born March 15th, 1969 in Laguna Beach, Christian Beamish has always been attracted to the water. His father introduced him to the ocean at a very young age and he has been surfing for more than 25 years. In 1987, after graduating high school, Christian joined the U.S. Navy and worked in a construction battalion on many overseas projects. His Navy travels have been a very important part of his development as a writer since he was exposed to many interesting places and people. The time he spent in Cape Verde with the Navy was the basis for the Paulo and Joaquim stories: the unique culture of the islands and the way the people there are so closely connected to the sea. Christian currently lives in San Clemente, California and has plans to build an 18-foot sailboat for the next stage of his ocean development.

Author's Note: About *Paulo Joins the Fleet*

In Cape Verde, the fishermen bring their boats onto the beach in the evening. Oftentimes the children seem to play around the boats and I imagined the day in Paulo's life when his father wanted him to learn how to fish. I liked the idea of the boy having to work hard and prove himself to his brother. Even though Paulo is still very much a boy at the end of the story, he has nevertheless made a big step in his life. I also noticed, while in Cape Verde, many children help their families by working and making a little extra income. For Paulo, Enrique and their father, fishing is what they must do to survive. I tried to make a story that had a nice setting, but that also showed how hard they have to work.

關於繪者

朱正明

1959 年次，現居台北市。
年幼好塗鴉；自高中時期即選讀美工科，業畢次年 (1979) 考取國立藝術專科學校美術科西畫組，1982 年以西畫水彩類第一名畢業。
求學時期除水彩、素描技法之外，並對漫畫、卡通之藝術表現形式頗有興趣，役畢後工作項度側重於卡通、漫畫、插畫。
1999 年驟生再學之念，並於次年考取國立師範大學美術研究所西畫創作組；2003 年取得美術碩士學位，該年申請入師大附中實習教師獲准，次年 2004 年取得教育部頒發之美術科正式教師資格證書，目前仍為自由工作者身分。

愛閱雙語叢書

(具國中以上英文閱讀能力者適讀)

祕密基地系列

Paulo, Joaquim and the Lighthouse Series

Christian Beamish 著

吳泳霈 譯

朱正明 繪

中英雙語，全套五本，附英文朗讀CD

①Crazy Joaquim 瘋子喬昆

②Paulo Joins the Fleet 第一次捕魚

③The Apology 保羅的道歉

④Homecoming 歸來

⑤The Blue Marlin Festival 藍馬林魚節

一段發生在西非的島嶼上，關於友誼與成長的故事。

在西非外海小島上的海邊漁村，矗立著一座燈塔。燈塔管理員是一個叫喬昆的獨居老人，村民們都誤以為他是個瘋子，但八歲的小男孩保羅卻和他成為忘年之交，並學到許多人生哲理。本系列五個溫馨且具啟發性的生活事件，紀錄喬昆和保羅的友誼。清新雋永的文字，配上細緻優美的插畫，值得您細細品味。

愛閱雙語叢書

世界故事集系列

你想知道，
如何用簡單的英文，
說出一個個耳熟能詳的故事嗎？

本系列改編自世界各國民間故事，
讓你體驗以另一種語言呈現
你所熟知的故事。

Jonathan Augustine 著
Machi Takagi 繪

Bedtime Wishes
睡前願望

The Land of the Immortals
仙人之谷

國家圖書館出版品預行編目資料

Paulo Joins the Fleet:第一次捕魚 / Christian Beamish 著;朱正明繪;吳泳霈譯.－－初版一刷.－－臺北市：三民，2005

面；　公分.－－(愛閱雙語叢書.祕密基地系列②)

ISBN 957-14-4331-X　(精裝)

1. 英國語言－讀本

524.38　　94012751

網路書店位址　http://www.sanmin.com.tw

© Paulo Joins the Fleet

──第一次捕魚

著作人　Christian Beamish

繪　者　朱正明

譯　者　吳泳霈

發行人　劉振強

著作財產權人　三民書局股份有限公司
臺北市復興北路386號

發行所　三民書局股份有限公司
地址／臺北市復興北路386號
電話／(02)25006600
郵撥／0009998-5

印刷所　三民書局股份有限公司

門市部　復北店／臺北市復興北路386號
重南店／臺北市重慶南路一段61號

初版一刷　2005年8月

編　號　S 805671

定　價　新臺幣貳佰元整

行政院新聞局登記證局版臺業字第〇二〇〇號

ISBN　957-14-4331-X　(精裝)